Shannon the Ocean Fairy was originally published
as a Rainbow Magic special. This version has
been specially adapted for developing readers
in conjunction with a Reading Consultant.

Reading Consultant: Prue Goodwin, lecturer in literacy and children's books.

ORCHARD BOOKS

This story first published in Great Britain in 2008 by Orchard Books
This Early Reader edition published in 2013 by Orchard Books
This edition published in 2016 by The Watts Publishing Group

10

© 2013 Rainbow Magic Limited.
© 2013 HIT Entertainment Limited.
Illustrations copyright Orchard Books 2013

HiT entertainment

A CIP catalogue record for this book is available from the British Library.

ISBN 978 1 40832 747 0

Printed in China

MIX
Paper from
responsible sources
FSC
www.fsc.org   FSC® C104740

The paper and board used in this book are made from wood from responsible sources

Orchard Books
An imprint of Hachette Children's Group
Part of The Watts Publishing Group Limited
Carmelite House, 50 Victoria Embankment, London EC4Y 0DZ

An Hachette UK Company
www.hachette.co.uk
www.hachettechildrens.co.uk

Shannon

the Ocean Fairy

by Daisy Meadows

ORCHARD

www.rainbowmagic.co.uk

The Fairyland Palace

Hawaiian Island

Surfing Waves

Dolphins

Baby Seahorses

← Coral

Jack Frost's
Ice Castle

Kirsty's
Gran's
House

Lighthouse

Cruiseliner

Café

ARCADES

Dock

Leamouth Pier

Sealions

Story One

The Enchanted Pearl

The Enchanted Pearl

Rachel Walker and her best friend Kirsty Tate raced across Leamouth Beach, laughing. They were on holiday together, staying with Kirsty's gran.

Down where the waves lapped onto the sand, the girls noticed a beautiful seashell. They gasped as a burst of pale blue sparkles fizzed out of it.

"Fairy magic!" Kirsty whispered. Their friendship with the fairies was a very special secret.

"Hello, girls," said a voice from the shell.

"It's the Fairy Queen!" Rachel grinned.

"We'd like to invite you to a special beach party," said the

Queen. "I hope you can come."

Suddenly, a rainbow shot out from the shell. When the two friends stepped onto it, they disappeared in a whirl of fairy magic.

The girls had been magically turned into fairies and were now standing on a different beach. It was crowded with fairies enjoying a party. King Oberon and Queen Titania welcomed them.

"The tide's coming in. Will the party end soon?" Rachel asked a nearby fairy. It was Shannon the Ocean Fairy! She was wearing a pink skirt and had a glittering starfish clip in her hair.

"No. The sea never comes

beyond Party Rock," Shannon smiled, pointing to a large boulder.

Suddenly, the party music stopped.

"The sea's coming in too far!" called Shannon.

"Something's wrong!"

"Jack Frost must be up to mischief again," said King Oberon. He asked Shannon to dive into the waves and look for clues in her underwater world.

Just then, a frog footman arrived. He told the king and queen that Jack Frost and his goblins had stolen the three Enchanted Pearls. Jack Frost hadn't been invited to the party, so he was determined to ruin it for everyone else.

Rachel and Kirsty exchanged an excited look. Whenever Jack Frost and his goblins caused trouble in Fairyland, the girls helped the fairies put things right.

When Shannon the Ocean

Fairy came fluttering back, King Oberon explained that Jack Frost had taken the pearls.

"My underwater world is in chaos!" Shannon cried.

The girls looked confused, so the little fairy explained.

"The Dawn Pearl makes sure that dawn comes each morning. It also affects the amount of water in the oceans. The Twilight Pearl makes sure that night falls every evening. The Moon Pearl controls the size of the waves."

"We'll help you find them!"
said Rachel, eager to help.

Shannon grinned and raised
her wand. As magic sparkles
whizzed around them, Rachel
and Kirsty shut their eyes. They
opened them a moment later
to find themselves standing on
the sandy seabed.

"We're under the sea!" Kirsty cried.

"It's magical!" Rachel laughed as she realised she was breathing and talking as if she was on land.

Shannon swam off. The two girls followed, whizzing through the water past colourful fish and coral caves. They were looking for clues. A moment later, three goblins swam towards them. One goblin was carrying a large rosy-pink pearl!

Rachel and Kirsty gazed at the pearl. It shone with a brightness that filled the ocean with light. At that moment, the goblins shot forward, holding the pearl like a torch.

"There's no treasure here!" the biggest one said to the others in disgust. They moved along the seabed, pearly light shining all around.

"Oh, no!" Shannon cried suddenly. She peered through a small opening in the nearby rock wall.

Rachel and Kirsty looked puzzled.

"This is the entrance to the Mermaid Kingdom," Shannon whispered. "Mermaids are very secretive and would hate their kingdom to be revealed!"

"Maybe we can tempt the goblins away with some treasure!" Kirsty suggested. "If you could magic up some gold coins, we could lay a trail."

"Good idea," said Shannon. "With the goblins trapped, maybe we can get the Dawn Pearl back." She waved her wand and a trail of shiny coins appeared in the sand, leading to a nearby coral cave.

Before long, the goblins came past. "Treasure!" yelled one of them, spotting a glinting coin.

Shannon, Rachel and Kirsty swam silently after the goblins as they picked up the coins one by one.

"Let's go!" Shannon whispered. The goblins shrieked with surprise when they saw the three fairies at the cave entrance.

"Please give me the Dawn Pearl," Shannon said politely.

"No way!" said one of the goblins. "You silly fairies can't make us!"

Just as the girls were wondering what to do, they saw lots of lobsters snapping at the goblins' ankles. The scared goblins backed away.

"Maybe we can't, but my
lobster friends can!" Shannon
smiled. "And they'll snap at
your ears and noses too."

"It's yours," the biggest of the
goblins squeaked, tossing the
Dawn Pearl to Shannon.

"Thank you," Shannon called. "And thank you, my lobster friends!" She waved her wand. In a burst of fairy dust, Shannon, Rachel and Kirsty were back on the empty beach in Leamouth.

Then the little fairy used her magic to make the girls human size again.

"I must take the Dawn Pearl back to Fairyland now," Shannon said. "Thank you for all your help. Don't forget, we still have the other two Enchanted Pearls to find!"

Rachel and Kirsty nodded and smiled as Shannon disappeared with the pearl in a whirl of fairy magic.

Story Two

Trouble
at Sea

Trouble at Sea

The next morning, Rachel, Kirsty and Gran set off for a walk along the seafront. "You go and explore," Gran said, looking up at the dark sky. "But don't be long – there's a storm on the way."

Gran sat down in The Starfish Café, while the two girls headed off along the pier. The sky was getting darker and darker even though the sun was shining. Kirsty and Rachel were just passing a small games arcade, when a machine began flashing.

"FREE PLAY," Rachel read aloud from the little screen.

The machine was full of soft toys. A metal claw hung above them. The claw, used to grab the toys, was operated by a lever. Rachel held the lever and moved the claw around, finally managing to grab a fluffy dolphin.

"Well done!" Kirsty cried.

Smiling, Rachel collected her prize from the machine. She gasped as a cloud of yellow sparkles burst out.

"Hello, girls!" Shannon the Ocean Fairy cried. "I need your help to find the Twilight Pearl. Now, quick, get out of sight!"

Rachel and Kirsty were very keen to help. They ducked behind the machine, where one flick of Shannon's wand transformed them into fluttering fairies. As they flew off the end of the pier, Shannon explained how nightfall was being disrupted everywhere. All because the Twilight Pearl was missing!

"Where are the goblins with the Twilight Pearl?" Kirsty asked.

"I think they're underwater.

Somewhere near here,"
Shannon replied. "That's why
it's so dark around the pier."

Then the little fairy tapped
her wand until the tip began to
sparkle brightly. "We'll use this
to light our way under the sea

and my fairy magic will help you breathe underwater," she said to the girls.

Suddenly, Shannon plunged into the sparkling blue ocean. Rachel and Kirsty followed.

"This way," Shannon said, darting through the water. It was becoming darker and darker.

Kirsty wondered how they were ever going to find the goblins. Even with Shannon's glowing wand, it was hard to see anything in the dark water.

"Wait here!" Shannon called. She swam off. Seconds later she returned with a school of beautiful dolphins behind her!

"The dolphins know the ocean better than anyone," Shannon explained. "Jump on, girls and hold tight. They're going to take us to the goblins." The excited girls clung on tightly as the dolphins zipped through the darkening sea.

After a while the dolphins slowed down. The girls could hear voices ahead.

"Goblins!" whispered Kirsty.

"I don't like the dark," one goblin whimpered. "I can't see!"

"Help!" the goblins called.

39

As the light from Shannon's wand shone through the black water, the goblins sneered at them.

"Give the Twilight Pearl back and we'll rescue you," Shannon offered.

"We're not scared!" The biggest goblin shivered.

"OK then. We'll go now, and take our light with us," Shannon said firmly.

"NO! Please stay," sobbed the goblin. "But we can't give the pearl back because we've

hidden it and now we can't
find it!"

"We know it's under a
really big rock," said another
goblin. They all looked sadly
at the hundreds of big rocks
around them.

Just then, Kirsty had a
brilliant idea.

"There's an old lighthouse by
the pier. Could your magic get
it working again?" she asked
Shannon.

"Maybe," the little fairy
replied. "Stay here!" she told the
goblins, as the three fairies shot
up into the sky.

"There's the lighthouse!"
Rachel cried. They flew in
through a broken window
just under the roof. Shannon
pointed her wand at the huge

broken lantern. Slowly, it lit up and began to turn.

"It's lighting up the sea," Kirsty cheered.

"Look!" Rachel called. She pointed at a silver shimmer in the water.

"The Twilight Pearl!" Shannon exclaimed. She whizzed out of the lighthouse.

Shannon dived into the glittering patch of sea. Rachel and Kirsty followed.

The pearl lay beneath a large rock. But as they gazed at its magical sheen, a goblin swam past and grabbed it!

Luckily, Shannon knew exactly what to do.

"If you don't give that pearl back," she called after him, "I'll turn the lighthouse off and leave you here in the dark."

The goblin was scared. "Take it!" he yelled. He swam away.

"Everyone in Fairyland will be so pleased to have the Twilight Pearl returned," Shannon said to Rachel and Kirsty. "But you must get back to Leamouth."

The three friends flew quickly

to the deserted end of the pier.
Shannon used some magic to
make Kirsty and Rachel human
size again.

"We just have the Moon Pearl to find now," Shannon reminded the girls. She gave them a big hug and disappeared in a cloud of fairy dust.

"I wonder where the goblins have hidden the Moon Pearl," Rachel said to Kirsty as they waved goodbye.

"I don't know, but I can't wait to find out!" replied Kirsty with a smile.

Story Three

Pearl Power

Pearl Power

The next day, Kirsty's gran was reading the newspaper.

"Oh, dear!" she said suddenly.

"What's the matter, Gran?" asked Kirsty. She and Rachel were busy packing their bags for a trip to the beach.

"There are reports of floods all around the world," Gran explained. "The sea is behaving very strangely."

Rachel and Kirsty looked worried. They knew it was because the Moon Pearl, which looked after the tides, was missing from Fairyland.

"Have fun, but make sure you're back in time for lunch," called Gran, as the girls hurried through the garden towards the beach. "And watch out for the tides!"

"I wonder if Shannon has found out where the goblins are hiding the Moon Pearl," said Rachel.

The girls had arrived on the empty beach. It was still very early so there weren't

many people about. They were
paddling in the clear water
when Rachel spotted a glass
bottle bobbing on the waves.

"Kirsty, look," she called, grabbing it as it floated past. "There's a piece of paper inside saying 'Open me!'"

As Kirsty pulled out the cork, Shannon the Ocean Fairy burst out of the bottle, along with a sparkling mist of sea-green bubbles!

"I need your help!" Shannon said quickly. "Fairyland is flooding, so we must find the Moon Pearl! I think it's at Breezy Bay Beach, with the naughty goblins."

"But how do we get there?" asked Kirsty.

"With fairy magic, of course!" Shannon smiled. She waved her wand and turned the girls into fairies.

"Follow me," she said, diving into the waves.

The three friends were carried through the ocean by a magical current. They whizzed through the clear water past colourful fish and coral reefs. Slowing down, they swam to the surface and popped out of

the sea beside a beautiful sandy
beach.

Suddenly, Rachel and Kirsty
could hear shouting and
laughter. They turned to see
a big wave heading towards
the beach. Riding on the wave
was a group of goblins on
colourful surfboards.

"They look so funny!"
Rachel whispered, giggling.
"But aren't they supposed to be
hiding with the Moon Pearl?"

"I think they've forgotten
about that!" Shannon grinned.

"The waves are enormous!" Kirsty gasped.

"Breezy Bay is famous for its big waves," Shannon said. "But I think the goblins are using the Moon Pearl to make the waves even bigger than usual."

"Then let's start searching!" Kirsty said eagerly.

The three friends ducked under the water again. They spotted a group of blue seahorses bobbing towards them. Shannon explained that they were friends of hers.

"We're looking for the Moon Pearl," she told the smiling creatures. "Have you seen it?"

The seahorses bounced up and down, looking very excited.

"We think so!" explained one

in a tiny voice. "Not far from here are two strange green creatures with flappy feet."

"And they're guarding a big white pearl," added another.

"Over there, over there!" chorused the rest.

"Thank you," Shannon said with a smile. "Come on, girls."

They swam off quickly. Before long, they spotted two goblins playing catch with a big creamy-white pearl. Darting behind a rock, the fairies worked out what to do.

"There are only two of
them," Shannon whispered.
"This is our chance!"

"Let's sneak over and grab
the pearl when it's in mid-air,"
Rachel suggested.

"Great idea!" Kirsty agreed.
When the goblin tossed the
pearl, Rachel swam forwards,
stretching out her arms to grab
it. But it was just too high for
her to catch!

"It's those annoying fairies!" yelled one goblin. The other goblin zoomed over and snatched the pearl away from Rachel's fingers. They shot off, using their huge flappy feet to help them go faster.

"After them!" Shannon cried.

But the goblins were getting away.

"They're too fast," Shannon panted. "It's no good." She stopped and looked at Rachel and Kirsty in dismay. "How are we ever going to get the Moon Pearl back?"

Just then, they heard a chorus of tiny voices say, "We can help! We can help!"

The friendly little seahorses were back!

"Jump on our backs," the

seahorses called, "and hold on tight!"

"They're fast!" Kirsty gasped, clinging onto her seahorse's neck as they zoomed away.

"There are the goblins," Rachel said, spotting them just ahead. "But how are we going to get the pearl?"

As they whizzed past a clump of seaweed, Kirsty had an idea.

"We could tie the goblins up!" she suggested.

"Good idea," said Shannon. With a burst of fairy magic, she knotted together some long strands of seaweed.

Quietly, the fairies and their seahorses sneaked up behind the goblins. Holding the long string of seaweed, they whizzed round and round the goblins.

"Help!" shrieked the goblins as the seaweed rope tightened around them.

Shannon took the Moon Pearl from their hands. "While you are freeing yourselves," she scolded, "have a think about how naughty you've been!"

After thanking the seahorses, Shannon showered herself and the girls with magic sparkles.

Suddenly, they were back in the air, flying over Fairyland.

"Look at the water!" Rachel gasped. Many of the toadstool houses were flooded.

Shannon swooped in through a window of the Fairyland Palace and returned the Moon Pearl to its proper place. Almost at once, the water began to disappear.

"Thank you for your help," said Shannon to the girls. She pointed her wand and a shower of fairy dust fell gently around them. When it cleared, they gasped with delight. They were each wearing a gold ring with a rosy pink pearl in the centre.

"They're beautiful!" said
Rachel and Kirsty together.

"Now, you should get back
to Gran's," said Shannon. She
waved her wand and a few
seconds later, the girls were
human size and back on
Leamouth Beach.

"What an amazing adventure!" Kirsty cheered. "This really has been the best holiday ever!"

**If you enjoyed this story,
you may want to read**

Flora the Fancy Dress Fairy
Early Reader

Here's how the story begins...

"What a beautiful place!"
Rachel Walker cried when
she saw McKersey Castle.
Her grown-up cousin Lindsay
was having a party there
to celebrate her wedding
anniversary and Rachel was
invited, along with her best
friend, Kirsty Tate.

"It's just like a fairytale
castle," Rachel said.

Kirsty grinned. She and
Rachel knew all about fairies
because they had met and
helped the fairies many times!

Inside the castle, Lindsay
showed them to their bedroom.

Rachel and Kirsty gasped
with delight when they saw
the huge room.

Lindsay pointed to a small door set opposite the beds.

"That door leads up to the battlements," she said. "Be careful if you go up there!"

As Lindsay hurried off, Rachel opened the little door and found a staircase winding upwards.

Suddenly a chilly gust of wind blew right down into the room.

"Look, there's ice all over the stairs!" Kirsty gasped.

The girls were curious,

so they climbed the steps,
holding onto the handrail.
The higher they got, the colder
they felt.

"My Icicle Party will be the
best fun ever!" snapped an icy
voice ahead of them.

Read
Flora the Fancy Dress Fairy
Early Reader
to find out
what happens next!

Learn to read with

RAINBOW
magic™

- Rainbow Magic Early Readers are easy-to-read versions of the original books

- Perfect for parents to read aloud and for newly confident readers to read along

- Remember to enjoy reading together. It's never too early to share a story!

Everybody loves Daisy Meadows!

'I love your books' – Jasmine, Essex
'You are my favourite author' – Aimee, Surrey
'I am a big fan of Rainbow Magic!' – Emma, Hertfordshire

Meet the first Rainbow Magic fairies

Can you find one with your name?
There's a fairy book for everyone at
www.rainbowmagicbooks.co.uk

Let the magic begin!

RAINBOW
magic™

Become a
Rainbow Magic
fairy friend and be the first to
see sneak peeks of new books.

There are lots of special offers and exclusive
competitions to win sparkly
Rainbow Magic prizes.

Sign up today at
www.rainbowmagicbooks.co.uk